I celebrated
World Book Day® 2025
with this gift from my
local bookseller and Scholastic.

....

....

SCHOLASTIC

WORLD BOOK DAY®

World Book Day's mission is to offer every child
and young person the opportunity to read and
love books by giving you the chance to have
a book of your own.

To find out more, and for fun activities including
video stories, audiobooks and book recommendations,
visit worldbookday.com

World Book Day® is a charity sponsored by
National Book Tokens.

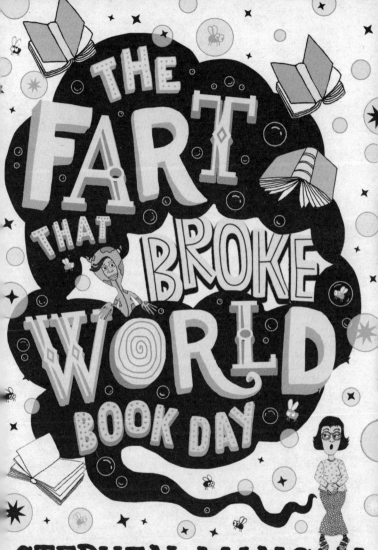

THE FART THAT BROKE WORLD BOOK DAY

STEPHEN MANGAN

ILLUSTRATED BY ANITA MANGAN

SCHOLASTIC

Published in the UK by Scholastic, 2025
Scholastic, Bosworth Avenue, Warwick, CV34 6XZ
Scholastic Ireland, 89E Lagan Road, Dublin Industrial Estate,
Glasnevin, Dublin, D11 HP5F

Text © Stephen Mangan, 2025
Illustrations © Anita Mangan, 2025

ISBN 978 07023 4063 5

A CIP catalogue record for this book is available from the British Library.

Printed in the UK
Paper made from wood grown in sustainable forests and other controlled sources.

MIX
Paper | Supporting
responsible forestry
FSC® C018072

1 3 5 7 9 10 8 6 4 2

www.scholastic.co.uk

CHAPTER ONE

My teacher Mr Brown-Stain (not his real name) kicked open the door of the classroom and we all fell silent. You didn't mess with Mr Brown-Stain.

As usual, he threw the pile of books he was holding on to his desk. As usual, he pulled off his green jacket with the leather elbow patches and hooked it on the back of the door. As usual, he kicked off his shoes and slid his disgusting damp and sweaty socks into the pair of tragic slippers he kept by the bin. And, as usual, he took out a crusty, yellowing handkerchief and blew his nose into it with four short sharp bursts.

But then he did something he had never done before.

Mr Brown-Stain walked down the middle of the classroom and – between the desks where Jezza Tuesday and Saskia Chintz usually sat – he sank to his knees and fell forward, his nose hitting the floor with a sickening *thunk*.

But he didn't cry out or moan or say **"ow"** or anything – he just lay there, face down and completely still.

I held my breath.

Nothing happened. No one dared to move. This might be a test and, as I've already said, you didn't mess with Mr Brown-Stain (his real name's Mr Bronson but he once had a brown sauce stain down the front of his shirt and we've called him

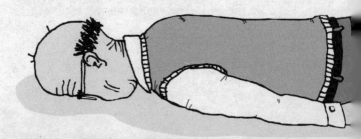

Mr Brown-Stain ever since – but not to his face, obviously).

Mr Brown-Stain had quite a temper on him. He once got so angry he picked up Leslie Grunt-Licker (that's actually her name – I know!) by the back of her school shirt and threw her out of the window. Our classroom is on the ground floor so she didn't fall eighty storeys to her death or anything. She just landed on the grass between the school and the path, but still you shouldn't really be throwing anyone out of windows, especially if you're their teacher and they're your pupil.

So we all just sat there, waiting to see what would happen, because none of us wanted to get thrown out of a window, but Mr Brown-Stain

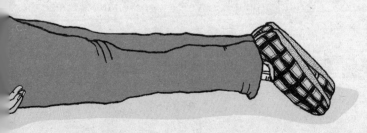

didn't move. As in: didn't move a single muscle –
it was really weird.

About three days passed and nothing
happened. OK, it was probably more like three
minutes, but that's a long time to be looking at
your teacher who's face down on the floor and no
one's talking or moving.

Then two things happened at once:

1. The door opened and the art teacher Miss
   Dollop (not her real name) burst in and
   gasped when she saw Mr Brown-Stain lying
   on the floor, and…

2. Mr Brown-Stain let out the longest and
   loudest fart you have ever heard in your life.
   I'm not kidding – this thing was **EPIC**. It
   should probably have its own Wikipedia page
   it was that monumental. If you've ever heard
   a ship sound its horn in the fog, then that's in

the kind of ballpark we're talking. Seriously, I reckon there's a chance I got ear damage it was that loud. I could feel it in my bones.

And that's when things began to move really fast.

But I'm getting ahead of myself, because I think I've started telling this story in the wrong place, so let's go back a bit…

CHAPTER TWO

That morning, I had arrived at school feeling annoyed because my beard was really itchy. So was the chunky blue jumper I was wearing. It was the beginning of March but way hotter than I'd ever remembered it being that early in the year, and my beard and jumper were making me sweaty and uncomfortable. I was convinced that if I lifted the big bushy black beard and looked underneath it, there would be a large red rash across my face.

At one point on the bus I'd drifted off into a daydream and started to imagine my beard was alive and had begun nibbling my face off. Daydreaming is something I do a lot.

You're thinking what a strange thing to be imagining. Don't worry – I think it's strange too, but that's what was going through my head, so go figure. We're not always in control of our minds. Well, I'm definitely not always in control of mine.

So, for a split second, I thought my fake beard was nibbling my face off and I yelled, "BEARD ATTACK! MY FACE!"

really, really loudly on a packed bus and everyone turned to look at me.

Willy Wonka, who was two rows in front of me, swizzled round, to see what the fuss was about. He was sitting next to Paddington Bear, who didn't turn round but then Paddington was very small. Willy Wonka and Paddington's mum did turn to look, though, and scowled at me like *I* was the weirdo when *she* was the one who'd given Paddington a bacon sandwich and *everybody* knows that Paddington eats marmalade sandwiches. He might even be a vegetarian (note to self: look up whether Paddington is a vegetarian or not) so that would make him eating a bacon sandwich even more wrong.

ANYWAY.

This was the first World Book Day I'd gone in as this character (did I say it was World Book Day? It was World Book Day) because if I'd known how horribly itchy this beard was going to be, I'd never have worn it. And hot – it was really hot. But I think I said that already.

So that was embarrassing (me shouting out) and, once I realized what was happening and where I was, I quickly looked around to see if I recognized anyone on the bus who might have heard me.

And there, at the back of the bus, was Mr Brown-Stain. He just stared at me without blinking. Right at me. It was … odd.

I tried to half smile at him. You know, a little smile to say, Yeah, I shouted out **"BEARD ATTACK! MY FACE!"** What am I like? But:

1. He just kept staring at me without blinking, in a way

that was freaking me out a bit…

2. Maybe he was wondering why I was on the bus on my own? Mum said I could get the bus to school, now that I was in Year 6, but I wasn't to talk to strangers.

3. Or perhaps Mr Brown-Stain couldn't even see that I was smiling because of the beard, so maybe he thought that *I* was staring at *him* without blinking.

Whatever. We looked at each other for too long and then I turned to the front. Willy Wonka was still staring at me. It made me feel even more self-conscious than I already was.

I nearly said, **"Why are you looking at me like that? Haven't you got an Oompa-Loompa you need to bother?"** but I decided not to, because Mum always says, **"If you can't say anything nice, don't say anything at all,"** but mainly because I noticed we were at my stop and the doors were opening and I'd better hurry or I'd be trapped on this bus until the next stop and be late for school.

So I jumped off the bus, glad to be out of there and relieved that the worst thing that could happen that day (me shouting out on a crowded bus about a face-eating beard) had already happened. But I can't tell you how wrong I was. My day was going to get **SO MUCH** worse and **SO MUCH** weirder.

"**All right, Gandalph?**" said Saskia Chintz to me as I walked into the playground.

"**You're kidding me, right?**" I said. "**Gandalph? I'm not Gandalph!**"

"**Oh, aren't you?**" she said.

"**No, Gandalph has a long white beard and long white hair that's swept backwards from his forehead, and he carries a big stick and sometimes smokes a pipe,**" I said.

"He's Hagrid!" shouted Leslie Grunt-Licker. "Because he's got a black beard and he's quite sweaty."

"I'm not Hagrid!" I protested. "Hagrid has a much bigger beard and long hair, and he doesn't wear knitted blue jumpers. And I'm only sweaty because this jumper is made of wool and I just ran from the bus stop to get away from Mr Brown-Stain and Willy Wonka."

"Are you Wolverine?" Saskia asked. She was dressed as Pippi Longstocking. Saskia dressed as Pippi Longstocking every year. Saskia *loved* Pippi Longstocking.

"Do me a favour!" I said. This was getting frustrating. "Wolverine has sharp metal claws."

"Well, your fingernails are pretty long," said Saskia.

I sighed.

"Mr Twit from *The Twits*?" suggested Jezza.

11

"Moses?" asked Saskia.

"Abraham Lincoln?"

"God?"

"I'M CAPTAIN HADDOCK!" I shouted. "CAPTAIN HADDOCK! Black beard, dark blue jumper equals Captain Haddock..."

They stared blankly at me.

"From *Tintin*," I explained. More blank expressions. "You must have heard of *Tintin*!"

At that point, Miss Dollop walked past us and I'm not quite sure how to put this, so I'm just going to come out with it – she farted. *SHE FARTED* – loudly, clearly, violently farted. It sounded like a wounded elk or the last groan of a dying bear or something in between those two. We looked at her, astonished. This was not like her *at all*. Mr Ritter the PE teacher, sure. He farted all the time and was all "pull my finger" this and "I should really change my ringtone" that, trying to be funny. And Saskia, it had to be said, was extremely farty too, probably because she loved Brussell sprouts, but hers were always silent but deadly, and out of politeness we'd never mention them. But Miss Dollop?! Never. She was quiet and shy, and blushed easily. She wore long skirts with tiny flowers on them and sandals, for goodness' sake. She ate couscous. She read hardback books. It had never even occurred to me that she was even *able* to fart. Jezza Tuesday was always telling me that *everyone* farts, even the king and prime ministers and the Pope and Beyoncé and BBC newsreaders, but if you'd asked me to list who were the most unlikely people in the world to fart, Miss Dollop would be near the top.

But fart she did. It was unmistakable. And loud. As my dad would have said, **"Looks like the Sorting Hat has picked another Hufflepuff."**

13

Miss Dollop said, **"Oops!"** and quickened her step a little. At least *I think* that's what she did but, to be honest, my brain buffered for a moment or two. I think all our brains buffered for a few seconds, trying to take in this bizarre chain of events.

Eventually Saskia said, **"Oh yeah, Tintin. It's a comic. Snowy the dog, right?"**

And then the four of us walked into assembly.

Assembly on World Book Day is always hilarious. You get loads of Harry Potters and Hermione Grangers – of course you do. You get your Pippi Longstockings, your Katniss Everdeens, your *Where's Wally?* Wallies, your Matildas and the random Cat in a Hat.

But there's always one kid who comes wearing a cardboard box over his head with squiggles drawn on it, and a pipe and a pair of wellies or something, and he's like, **"Oh yeah, I'm Prince Bernard Toaster-Pigeon from the medieval Italian book *The Cardboard Box of Destiny*, volume twelve."** I mean, not that *exactly*, but you get the drift.

And I have to say I like those people who do something a little out of the ordinary. Who try to be original. And you've always got to admire someone who's read a lot of different books. That's all good.

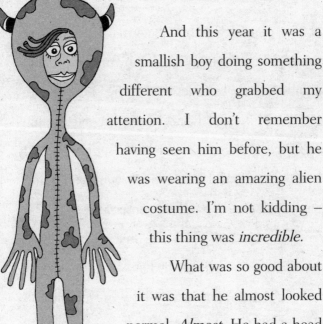

And this year it was a smallish boy doing something different who grabbed my attention. I don't remember having seen him before, but he was wearing an amazing alien costume. I'm not kidding – this thing was *incredible*.

What was so good about it was that he almost looked normal. *Almost*. He had a head and a body and legs and two eyes and all the rest of it, but everything was just a little *out*.

A little freaky-deaky.

His neck was just a bit too thin, his head was just a bit too large, his arms were just a bit too long. The effect was *out of this world*.

The best thing was his hair, which was kind

of like normal hair but if normal hair was the thickness of spaghetti. Dark brown, side parting, combed neatly, but a lot thicker than normal hair. It was so unusual I had to stop myself leaning right over to have a closer look. But that would have been weird if he'd turned round and found me inspecting his hair from close range.

The hair was the thing that grabbed your attention first (I mean, who has hair the thickness of spaghetti?!) and then you began to notice all the other odd things about him. It was genius and I had no idea how he'd done it.

"Who's that?" I whispered to Jezza, pointing to the kid. Jezza shrugged and went back to staring at the ceiling with his mouth open – Jezza's favourite position. I reckon Jezza might have been a gecko in a former life: one of those that just sits there in the sun and doesn't move for hours at a time.

"Who are you?" I whispered to the kid.

"I'm Ronnie," he whispered back.

"What book's that from?" I hissed.

"It's not from a book," he said. "It's my name."

"Oh, no – I meant what character have you come as?"

"You're Captain Haddock," he said, ignoring my question. "Best friend of the Belgian newspaper reporter Tintin. Haddock gets angry a lot and

says things like 'blue blistering barnacles'. I've read most of the stories. I think *Tintin in Tibet* is my favourite."

And with that Ronnie turned to face the front, as if to say, *This conversation is over.* What he lacked in height, he more than made up for in attitude.

At that moment, the Head walked in and joined the other teachers. I noted Miss Dollop come in looking her usual shy self, like she'd just finished doing something wholesome, like donating money to famine relief or knitting herself a new teapot warmer or adopting twelve orphaned kittens. She sat next to Mr Ritter, crossed her ankles and placed her hands on her lap. She didn't look up once but kept her gaze down towards the floor. Was she embarrassed about the massive fart she'd let rip earlier?

"**Good morning,**" said Mrs Surely, the

headmistress, "and may I wish you all a happy World Book Day."

She scanned the room, taking in all the various outfits and costumes.

"I can see that you've all been reading some wonderful books and that you've gone to great efforts." Her eyes landed on Scarlett O'Mara in the front row.

"Scarlett, you've come as Scarlett O'Hara again." Scarlett O'Mara had indeed come as Scarlett O'Hara – she did so every year.

"And, Jenny," she continued, picking out another girl in the front row, "have you come as the witch from *Room on the Broom*?"

"No, Miss," said Jenny, her face reddening. "I forgot

21

to get an outfit this year. This is what I always look like."

Awkward.

"Well," stammered Mrs Surely, "you look lovely. Whoever you have come as. Or whoever you have not come as."

CHAPTER THREE

The dressing-up bit of World Book Day is good, but the best bit is *all the books* and I didn't always think like that, trust me.

Books used to feel like homework, like hard, horrible homework. I got *so bored* reading them that I thought I was going to fall asleep as soon as I opened the first page. Even *looking* at a book made me yawn.

I think it was partly because I was being made to read them, whether I wanted to or not, and I don't like being told what to do – I never have. If someone tells me to sit down, I want to stand up. If someone tells me to be quiet, I want to shout. If someone tells me to eat my dinner, I want to get up from the table and run a mile. I like things to be my idea.

I'm not saying this is a good thing, but it's just the way I am.

So, if someone gave me a book, I wouldn't read it, partly because I figured it would be boring, and partly because it hadn't been my idea to get it. That changed, though, because of a book my Uncle Esteban gave me. He's Spanish and married to my Aunt Louise and he looks a bit like the donkey from *Shrek*, but he's nice and he gave me a book for my birthday and said, **"I think you and this book will get along"** – like the book was a person. Which it wasn't. It was a book.

I didn't read it.

23

Then the librarian at school saw the book in my bag and said, **"Oh that's a great book for you – you'll really get on with it."** Again, as if the book had a personality like a person, and this time I thought, *OK, if two people reckon I'd like this book, I might as well try it*. And I did and I **LOVED IT**. That changed everything.

And I realized that, yes, books are like people.

Some people are annoying, some people are boring, some people are funny, some people are interesting. Some people you can't stand as soon as you lay eyes on them, some people you want to hero-worship, some people are all right, some people are your best friends. People are all different, and some you like and some you don't.

You wouldn't give up on *all* people just because you met *one* boring one. Or even ten boring ones. Because you know that there are *other* people who you will really like and who will make you laugh and who you'll want to hang out with. You just have to find them.

It's exactly the same with books.

Yeah, some books are boring or don't interest you or you simply don't get. But the ones that you *do* get – **"Oh, Lordy! Lordy! Lordy!"** as my grandad used to say. He also used to say **"Oh sweet green patooties!"** which I think means the same kind of thing, but who knows? Grandad was always saying stuff like that, but he was kind and he made me laugh and always talked to me like I was a grown-up, not a kid.

ANYWAY.

Finding a good book is like meeting the best person ever – and I mean the best person ever *in your opinion*, because sometimes you meet someone you like and who you think is funny/nice/interesting/brilliant or whatever but everyone else doesn't get them. And that's OK. You're the one hanging out with the book or the person, so you're the one who has to like them.

Anyway, what I'm trying to say is that I now *get it* when it comes to books, and I'm glad I do. Some of the best times I've had have been spent reading a great book.

CHAPTER FOUR

After assembly, I went to the school library to look at the new book display put up by Mr Wojciechowski (he's the librarian I was talking about, and he's Polish, or at least his dad was and you say his name *Voy-check-off-ski* – he gets annoyed if you say it wrong). Mr Wojciechowski

(*Voy-check-off-ski*) is grumpy nearly all the time, and his shoulders are always coated in a thick layer of dandruff, but he knows *a lot* about books. I reckon he's read nearly all of them. It certainly feels like that. If I pick up any book in the library, he'll be all, **"Oh yes, that's an amusing detective story about a fish that solves murders"** or whatever. The best thing you can say to him is, **"I liked *this book* but I didn't like *that* book, so what book do you think I should try next?"** Then he'll run it through the vast memory banks in his head and say, **"Oh, you should try *this*,"** and show me a book. He doesn't always get it right, but he does a lot of the time. It saves me from having to pick books at random and hope for the best. The only thing is, don't get too close to him when he's recommending a book if there's a draft in the room, otherwise you'll get a face full of dandruff.

So there I was, checking out some of the books

27

he'd laid out on the table, when that spaghetti-haired alien-costume kid came in and marched up to Mr Wojciechowski's desk, put down the holdall he was carrying, and said,

"Good morning, teacher. It's Ronnie here. May I place my holdall on the floor? Are you enjoying a cup of morning tea?"

I thought two things:

1. How funny that a bag is called a 'holdall' because it *holds all* the things, and wouldn't it be great if everything was named like that? We wouldn't have

'beds', we'd have 'sleeptables'. We wouldn't have 'spoons', we'd have 'smallfoodbowlswith-handles' and so on, which reminds me of something else I thought the other day – that tables are pretty much just floor on stilts.

2. This kid is brilliant at being an alien, because he's kind of speaking like a normal person but everything is just a little bit wrong. He's speaking like someone who has learned English like a computer would learn English.

Can I just say at this point that my mind tends to bounce around all over the place so sorry if that's confusing. You know Tigger from *Winnie-the-Pooh*? My body doesn't act like Tigger but my brain does, boinging around all over the shop. If you have a brain that thinks of things all neatly and in a row, I hope the way my brain works isn't doing your head in. (*Doing your head in* is such a weird phrase when you stop and think about it. Doing. Your head. In. What does that even mean?)

ANYWAY.

Mr Wojciechowski looked up at Ronnie and said, "I don't drink tea."

Ronnie blinked a few times then said, "How interesting, teacher. Do you drink another liquid in its place?"

"Um," said Mr Wojciechowski, starting to look a little annoyed. He was reading (he was always reading) and everyone knew not to bother him when he was reading. "I drink coffee until lunchtime, then I drink water. Is there something I can help you with?"

"You drink coffee until lunchtime," said Ronnie. "The time now is 11.35 a.m. so it is within your coffee-drinking window. Do you have a cup of coffee in progress?"

Mr Wojciechowski sighed deeply and, grabbing the lapels of his jacket, gave them a flick, sending clouds of dandruff into the air. This was a dangerous thing to be close to. Once, he'd flicked the dandruff off his shoulders and a random breeze had blown a clump right up my nose. Even though I blew my nose about seventy times afterwards, I swear some is still up there.

Ronnie didn't seem to notice, though, and waited patiently for a reply. Eventually Mr Wojciechowski said, **"Shouldn't you be getting to your next class now ... er...?"**

"Ronnie."

"Ronnie." Mr Wojciechowski gave him a closer look. **"That's an amazing costume, Ronnie. Congratulations."**

"Thank you," said Ronnie. **"It is for World**

Book Day. Today is World Book Day, and on World Book Day children everywhere talk about books and some dress up as characters from books they have enjoyed."

"Yes," said Mr Wojciechowski. "I know."

Ronnie blinked.

And then blinked a few more times.

There was a very awkward silence.

"Maybe I will have a cup of coffee," said Mr Wojciechowski.

He got up and went to the kettle on a table in the corner and switched it on. Ronnie followed him, glancing at me as he went. I realized I was just standing there staring, so I picked up the nearest book and pretended to read.

"You are holding the book upside down," said Ronnie, and he was right – I was.

32

"Yes, sometimes I read books like that," I said, but I felt silly because that was clearly not true.

Then nobody spoke for a while. I pretended to read. Mr Wojciechowski waited for the kettle to boil. Ronnie stood there blinking in that exaggerated way he did.

Mr Wojciechowski made his coffee, took it back to his desk, and Ronnie followed him over. Only when Mr Wojciechowski had sat down did Ronnie say, "Do you have the book *The Wind in the Willows* by Kenneth Grahame published in 1908?"

"*The Wind in the Willows?*" Mr Wojciechowski repeated.

"Yes," said Ronnie. "Published in 1908. It is an amusing story about a mole, a rat and a badger as they help a toad. They are not humans, but they dress and speak just like humans."

"Yes, I know *The Wind in the Willows*. Of

course," said Mr Wojciechowski, and he got up to fetch it.

"**I am grateful,**" said Ronnie. He was doing an excellent job of speaking strangely. Who says "**I am grateful**"? It's the sort of phrase I can imagine Dracula saying as he sinks his teeth into your neck to suck your blood. "**I am grateful for the delicious neck you are offering me. Mwah ha ha!**" *Slurp, slurp, slurp.*

I heard a tiny *plop* and saw Ronnie's hand hovering over Mr Wojciechowski's coffee cup. What had just happened? Had Ronnie dropped something into Mr Wojciechowski's drink? Why would he do that?

Ronnie looked over at me, did some blinking, smiled, picked up his holdall and walked out of the library, saying, "**See you in twenty-three minutes, Mr Wojciechowski.**"

Mr Wojciechowski, who was returning with

The Wind in the Willows in his hand, looked confused.

"I thought you wanted..." He held up the book, but saw that Ronnie had gone.

Mr Wojciechowski looked at me, and I looked back at him. I wondered if I should say anything about the *plop.* But Mr Wojciechowski sighed heavily, grabbed his lapels and, before he could flick a dandruff cloud in my direction, I left the library.

That turned out to be a mistake.

CHAPTER FIVE

I had a lesson to go to. Art. Miss Dollop. I haven't told you why she's called Miss Dollop, have I? It's because she always overuses the word **"dollop"**, especially whenever we're using paints.

"Jezza, you could add a dollop of yellow to

that blue and it'll make green."

"Saskia, you've dropped a dollop of black on your skirt."

"I had scones with a large dollop of cream and a large dollop of jam, and it was delicious!"

It's her favourite word. So she became Miss Dollop. She doesn't know she is Miss Dollop – we call her Miss Stanton when she's listening, although once Jezza accidentally called her Miss Dollop to her face, and me and Leslie got the giggles so badly (shoulders shaking, tears coming out of our eyes, snot bubbling from our nostrils, you know what that's like) that we got sent to Mrs Surely for a telling-off. We couldn't stop. And the more embarrassing it got, the more we giggled. It was the worst we've ever giggled. Even worse than the time Jezza accidentally called Mr Streather **"Mummy"**.

I was finding it difficult to concentrate, as I kept thinking about Ronnie and his odd behaviour, especially him saying, very specifically, **"See you in twenty-three minutes, Mr Wojciechowski."** I kept an eye on the clock, and when twenty minutes had passed, I asked Miss Dollop if I could go to the loo. I ran down the stairs, along the science corridor and into the library.

Ronnie was there, just as he'd promised. He was bent over and rummaging through his holdall. Mr Wojciechowski was looking irritated by the noise Ronnie was making. This was Mr Wojciechowski's reading time, and anything that disturbed that got on his nerves.

Ronnie found what he was searching for and pulled it out from the holdall. It was some sort of device. It was a bit like a small vacuum cleaner – a nozzle at one end, a bag in the middle and a control panel full of dials and flashing lights near the handle. It looked expensive. Ronnie pressed a few buttons on the control panel, then walked over to Mr Wojciechowski, all the while keeping his eye on the clock that hung over the Science Fiction bookshelf.

"**Ronnie,**" began Mr Wojciechowski, but didn't get any further. A look of alarm flashed across his face. He gripped the sides of the desk and made to stand, but changed his mind and quickly sat down again.

Ronnie stood behind Mr Wojciechowski's chair, pointing the nozzle of his machine towards Mr Wojciechowski's bum.

"**I,**" stammered Mr Wojciechowski, "**I...**
I... Look, would you–"

His face creased, his eyes closed, he slapped the desk with his right hand, he half stood, sat, stood again, muttered something I couldn't make out, then unleashed a long, loud and sonorous fart. It lasted, I'm not kidding, about two minutes. I promise you *two whole minutes*, which, and I know I don't need to tell you this, is *way* longer than any fart has any right to be. And it was loud. You know the noise big ships make when they are coming into harbour? That loud. Which, and I don't need to tell you this either, is way louder than a fart ought to be. Lorries sometimes have horns that are incredibly loud. It was like that. For two minutes.

And for the entire two minutes Ronnie stood behind Mr Wojciechowski, his nozzle pointed at Mr Wojciechowski's bottom, while he kept a close eye on the control panel on his machine. What on earth was Ronnie doing?!

Mr Wojciechowski looked more than a little surprised but seemed unable to move. I was frozen to the spot. After a while, I began to wonder if I was in danger from choking or poisoning or suffocation or some other fart-related issue, but to my great relief I smelled nothing and seemed to be breathing normally.

When finally, *finally* it finished, Ronnie pressed another couple of buttons on the control panel, put the machine back into his holdall and marched out of the library, looking quite cross. Which I suppose was fair enough, as a librarian had, you know, farted at him for two whole minutes, but if it had annoyed him, why did he just stay there and watch it happen?

I opened and closed my mouth a few times, unable to think of anything to say, and then turned and left the library too. I was in a bit of a daze, but whether that was caused by surprise or by inhaling noxious fumes from Mr Wojciechowski's bottom, I couldn't say.

Mr Wojciechowski sat there breathing heavily. Whether he was embarrassed by what had just happened or was merely relieved to be shot of all that gas was hard to tell.

CHAPTER SIX

As I got to Miss Dollop's classroom door, Ronnie came running towards me down the corridor. I held out my hand to stop him.

"Good morning," he said. **"I am hurrying."**

"Right," I said. **"I can see that."**

"Goodbye," he said, and went to move off.

"But, Ronnie," I said, **"what's going on? What just happened? That was so weird."**

Ronnie stood there blinking at me but said nothing.

"What was that thing you were pointing at Mr Wojciechowski?"

Ronnie blinked some more.

"How can we ever face him again now we've seen him fart for ages right in front of us? It's so embarrassing!" I said. Ronnie just blinked.

I knew I needed to get back into Miss Dollop's art class, but I had so many questions. Ronnie, however, said nothing.

Then I noticed that he was holding a white holdall. I was sure the holdall he had in the library had been black.

Hadn't it?

My head swam. Was I imagining things?

"Your bag…" I began, but Ronnie suddenly said, "Goodbye," and ran off down the corridor.

Confused and bewildered, I pushed open the door of the art classroom.

"You took your time," said Miss Dollop. "Is everything OK?"

I looked at her blankly.

"I have diarrhoea," I lied, and I turned and ran out of the classroom again.

I galloped down the main staircase but couldn't see Ronnie anywhere. Had he turned left towards the gym or right towards the dining hall? Shouldn't he be in class himself? What was going on with the black/white holdalls? Had he dropped something into Mr Wojciechowski's coffee? And what was the strange machine he had pointed at Mr Wojciechowski's farting bottom?

I ran towards the gym but found no trace of Ronnie. The hallways were quiet and empty as lessons were in full swing. It felt odd and exciting to be wandering around on my own, but I couldn't shake the feeling that I shouldn't be out here.

Doubling back past the staircase, I checked everywhere I could think of that wasn't a classroom, even peering round the door into the empty science lab, which was *definitely* not somewhere I was allowed with no teacher present. Nothing.

I tried the toilets, but they were deserted. I locked myself in one of the cubicles so I could think.

Was I overreacting? Was I missing an obvious explanation? Had the whole thing been some sort of practical joke played on Mr Wojciechowski by a new kid? It was strange that I'd never seen Ronnie at this school before...

The main door to the toilets opened and I panicked. Even though a toilet was exactly the place you'd expect to find a boy with diarrhoea, I didn't want to have to explain myself to anyone.

I could hear footsteps and I found myself standing up on the toilet bowl, so that if anyone checked under the door of my stall they wouldn't see any feet

and would assume it was empty.

It was a move I'd seen on a detective show on telly and was pretty pleased with myself for thinking of it.

The footsteps walked slowly down the line of cubicles until they got to my door. Whoever it was pushed against it. *Why?!* I held my breath, balancing on the toilet bowl. The door rattled a few times, there was a pause, and the person moved on, slipping into a cubicle a few to my left and locking the door.

I wondered what to do and decided to wait until whoever it was had gone, then I would go back up to my art class and get on with my lessons. I was beginning to wonder if I *had* overreacted. So Mr Wojciechowski had farted and Ronnie had acted strangely? It was World Book Day – everything was always a little different on World Book Day. So Ronnie had two holdalls – a black and a white one – so what? And perhaps I had freaked him out by bombarding him with all my questions, and that's why he scuttled off. And now here I was standing on a toilet hiding, but from whom exactly? I reckoned the only truly odd thing around here might be me and that I needed to get a grip.

Another person came into the toilets and

made a little kind of chirrup noise as he walked along the front of the cubicles. It's a difficult sound to describe. I hadn't heard anything like it before. If you imagine a bird sound but made by a bad computer program... I can't think of a better way to put it. Computers are great, but they don't always get it quite right because they aren't human, and sometimes logic and computer programs can only take you so far. The other day I asked my computer what **"sixty-three"** was in German and this came up on the screen:

63

Which is not the answer I was looking for, but, like I said, to a computer it probably made sense.

Anyway, this chirruping person chirruped a couple of times and my first thought was, *That's an unusual noise*, but I wasn't completely amazed by it or anything. I just thought that it was a little unusual, but then the *other* person who had come in earlier and gone into the cubicle along from me made *exactly the same sound* and my blood ran cold. I swear I felt instantly both freezing cold and also too hot. I was scared. I don't scare easily: I'm fine with terrifying rollercoasters, horror films and spiders, rats and snakes, but in that moment a bolt of fear tore right through me like boiling water through ice cream.

Then they both started doing the chirruping noise at the same time.

Chirrup. Chirrup. Chirrup. Chirrup ChirrupChirrupChirrup.

The chirrups came faster and faster. Each one sounded identical and they didn't get louder or change in any way, except that there were more and more of them. They came so thick and fast that it sounded like there were too many to be coming from just two people.

ChirrupChirrupChirrupChirrup

ChirrupChirrupChirrupChirrup.

I wanted desperately to jump down from the toilet and look underneath the stalls to see how many pairs of feet there were – it *couldn't* just be two people making that noise! But I couldn't risk making a sound and being discovered. How would I explain standing on the rim of the toilet like that?

ChirrupChirrupChirrupChirrup

ChirrupChirrupChirrupChirrup.

Then suddenly the chirruping stopped.

"... are correct," said a voice that sounded like Ronnie's. **"We should use their language in case of toilet arrival."**

"Affirmative," said the other one, and *he also sounded like Ronnie!*

Of course! I thought. They are *twins* and they have a *special* language they invented that only they understand! I had heard of twins who talked to each other in made-up code or could understand each other without even using words. I always thought it sounded like a pretty cool thing, to be able to talk so that only one other person in the world understood you.

"**We need more,**" continued the first. "Much more."

Need much more what?

"**The next eating event is at what they call 'lunch'. We must hit our target then or it will be difficult to maintain operational anonymity.**"

They did talk in a strange way. **"Eating event"**? What were they planning for lunch?

"Affirmative," said the other. **"Shall we take one as back-up?"**

Take one? Take one what? And where?

"Yes, my readings suggest Apple Seedy Extended Socks has optimal capacity."

Who? What?

The door to the toilet opened and someone came in. That seemed to stop the conversation between the twins and everything went quiet. All I could make out was someone leaving, someone else washing their hands and then leaving, and finally the cubicle door down from mine opening and whoever was in it (one of the twins, I guess) leaving too.

I was alone.

I jumped down from the toilet and rushed for the door.

CHAPTER SEVEN

I was going to follow the twins to try and find out what they had been talking about.

They were nowhere to be found and I looked *everywhere*. As I passed Miss Dollop's art class again, I thought I should stick my head in to tell her that I still had a dodgy tummy. I liked Miss Dollop and didn't want to annoy her. I opened the door and said, "**Still feeling really rough, Miss.**" Then I noticed Ronnie sitting in my seat, next to Saskia!

"**Oh, sorry to hear that,**" said Miss Dollop. "**I should take you to the nurse, get you a dollop of medicine.**"

"**I'm suddenly feeling a lot better,**" I said. "**In fact, I feel fine now.**"

"**Oh,**" said Miss Dollop, clearly confused – and who could blame her?

"Yes, my tummy feels great!" I said, and then went to take the seat behind Ronnie.

"We have a new pupil," Miss Dollop explained to me.

"Yes, we met," I said. "Hello, Ronnie."

"Her name is Bonnie," said Miss Dollop. "Now let's get on with your drawings, please. We're drawing our favourite scene from a book. Jezza, you could do with a dollop more red in yours, I think."

Bonnie looked *identical* to Ronnie, not just twin-identical but so similar it was amazing. As I passed her, Saskia gave me a look, but I couldn't work out what she meant by it. I took a peek at Saskia's drawing: it was of Pippi Longstocking lifting her horse with one hand. Of course it was – Saskia loved that scene. I glanced at Bonnie's: her drawing was exactly the same as Saskia's! *Exactly.* Saskia gave me another pointed look as I sat down.

I busied myself with drawing for a few minutes as I tried to work out what was going on and what to do. I drew Captain Haddock getting shocked by an electric eel. I was reminded of that scene by Saskia's (and Bonnie's) drawing of a horse, because in the Tintin book *Picaros* they say that a fully grown electric eel is so powerful that it is able to stun a horse with a single charge of electricity. The bit when Captain Haddock is given an electric shock by the eel is really funny, so I drew that as I thought about Bonnie.

Why would she draw the same thing as Saskia? She couldn't also be a Pippi Longstocking fan, could she? Surely she was into science fiction if she had come dressed as an alien? Why hadn't she drawn something from a science fiction story?

I tried to think of reasons why I would copy someone else like that, and the only thing that came to my mind was that I'd copy someone if I couldn't think of anything to draw myself. Like if I hadn't done my homework so had no idea what I was expected to do, or if I'd been daydreaming about nibbling beards and hadn't been listening in class so didn't know where to begin.

The logical conclusion could only have been that Bonnie *didn't know a single scene from any books to draw*. If she did, she would have drawn it, wouldn't she? And the only reason you wouldn't know any scene from any book would be:

1. If you had never read a single book in your life.
2. You had zero memory, so as soon as you read something it went completely out of your head for ever.

"What are you drawing, Bonnie?" I asked.

Bonnie turned and blinked at me. "A scene from a book."

"Which book?"

"The book I enjoyed very much."

"What is it called?"

"It is called the name of the book. It has a four-legged beast and a female human."

"And it's called..."

"Yes, it's called. Goodbye."

Then she turned back to her drawing. Before I could ask another question, the bell for the end of the lesson went off and everyone stood up to leave.

"I'm coming with you," I heard Bonnie say to Saskia. "To the lunch event."

"Okaaaay," said Saskia slowly, and she threw me a look that I understood immediately as: *Don't leave me alone with Bonnie – she's a bit odd.*

CHAPTER EIGHT

Jezza and Leslie walked with us to lunch. No one spoke. As we crossed the playground, I spotted Ronnie running towards the playing fields and knew I needed to follow him. *He had both holdalls with him.*

"Jezza!" I hissed. "Come with me!" Then I ran off in Ronnie's direction.

As we fled, I heard Saskia say, "Oh great. Thanks a bunch, guys."

"A bunch of what?" said Bonnie. "And why are you thanking it?"

We followed Ronnie to the football pitches and watched as he ducked through the big hedge that ran along the furthest pitch.

"Let's go round the other way," I whispered to Jezza.

"What are we doing?" he asked me, out of

57

breath. **"Did he steal your bags?"**

I shook my head.

"Can't explain now," I said. **"We should see where he's going. I think he's got Mr Wojciechowski's fart in there."**

"I'm sorry – what?" said Jezza, but I didn't have the time to go into all the whys and wherefores and whatnots I'd seen that morning. I knew I had to find out where Ronnie was heading, so I sprinted off to the other end of the hedge.

"I'm going back," called Jezza. **"I don't think my parents would understand if I got expelled for going through the hedge to look for Mr Wojciechowski's fart."** And off he ran. You couldn't really blame him, could you?

Now, you need to know something about this hedge, because at our school this hedge was a big deal and there aren't many *hedges* you can say that about, are there? The history books are not full of stories of kings, queens, explorers and *hedges*, are they? Hedges don't usually play a big part in most great stories, but let me tell you this *hedge* plays an important part in this one. It was strictly forbidden to go through this hedge or round this hedge, because there was a railway line on the other side of it and Mrs Surely was always reminding us how dangerous it was. The railway line wasn't right next to the hedge: there was the hedge, a gap, a fence and then the railway line, so it wasn't as if I was in danger of being run over by a train as soon as I stepped behind the hedge, but it was definitely and properly and completely out of bounds to go *behind the hedge*. Only a year ago, Gemma Jamshed had been expelled for doing exactly what I was about to do (she hid there for a whole morning to miss double maths and PE), so I understood when Jezza stopped and said he was going back.

I knew it was a dangerous and stupid thing to do, but I *had* to see what Ronnie was up to, so I shrugged and kept on going. I was breathing heavily from running and could feel my heartbeat banging hard against my ribs. I pushed branches out of my way, cutting my right hand on a thorn as I did so. The hedge was old and wide, and it was a struggle to get past it.

Peeking through to the other side, I couldn't believe my eyes at what was there. Even now I have a difficult time describing it. Let me think…
It was a big *thing*, about the size of three double-decker buses side by side, so *really* big. It was totally black – so black that it was hard to see it properly. A black like I'd never seen before. So black that your eyes got a bit bored looking at it and they became easily distracted by other

stuff nearby (*A tree! A plant!*) and you'd have to refocus on the big black thing. Light seemed to disappear into it and not come out again. It was curvy except for two (black) tubes at the bottom that it was sitting on. The main top bit looked like someone had sat on a whale and squashed it. It had no windows, no doors. It was... I can hardly say it because it still sounds wrong... It was... It had to be... It could only have been... It must have been ... a *spaceship*.

Look, I understand if you just threw this book across the room and said, **"A spaceship?! What is he talking about?"** but I know what I saw. And *that* was a spaceship. The thing that sealed the deal for me (and maybe I should have mentioned this straight away) was that there were about sixty Ronnies all around it. *SIXTY.* All completely identical. So now tell me I was making a mistake...

One of the Ronnies was carrying two holdalls and I guessed that must have been the one we'd been chasing. He put them down on the ground, opened them up and, from each one, pulled out a device like I'd seen at the library. He passed one of the machines to another Ronnie who pulled down a flap on the side of the ship and attached the device to it.

There was a loud sucking sound, and the bag at the bottom of the device went limp, as though it had been emptied. The two Ronnies looked at what I guessed was a gauge beside the flap. The line on it hadn't risen very much.

They were making the teachers fart and then collecting the farts and putting the farts into, presumably, a tank on their ship.

But why?

Were farts precious in their world? Was this like us going to a different planet, picking up lots of diamonds or gold and taking them back home to sell for lots of money? Were they fart miners?

Or did they need the farts for some personal use? Perhaps they breathed farts in the same way we breathe air, so these tanks were like oxygen tanks for them and they needed lots for the journey home?

Or were the teachers' farts fuel? Could that

be possible? Had they run out of fuel and needed our farts to power their spaceship home again?

When both devices had been emptied, the first Ronnie put them back in the holdalls and said, "**Lunch.**"

All the other Ronnies started repeating the word: "**Lunch, lunch, lunch, lunch, lunch.**" The effect was unnerving, and after a few moments I felt fear creeping back into my bones and an incredible urge to get out of there.

Lunch. If their plan involved doing something at lunch, I had to get back to warn everyone. Lunch was happening *right now.*

CHAPTER NINE

I burst into the dining hall to find the place full but noisy as usual. We ate at long tables and sat on long benches. Bonnie – or whatever her/his/

its real name was – was sitting rather too close to Saskia. Jezza and Leslie were there too.

I slid in next to Jezza and, keeping a careful eye on Bonnie, whispered, **"What's going on?"**

"Ronnie," he whispered. **"The one we were chasing, he came back and helped to serve the food for the teachers. Then he left."**

"Did he drop anything into their food?" I asked, thinking of the *plop* I'd heard when Ronnie was standing by Mr Wojciechowski's (*Voy-check-off-ski* – you're welcome) coffee.

Jezza shrugged.

"And Bonnie?" I hissed.

"Hasn't left Saskia's side."

The teachers ate separately from us at a big table. I glanced over. Ronnie had served them their food? That was *very* suspicious.

"Bonnie is an alien," I said into Jezza's ear as quietly as I could. **"And so is Ronnie."**

66

Jezza looked at me for a couple of seconds and said, **"I think you having the runs has done something to your head. Did you poo your brain out?"**

That kind of comment didn't deserve a response, but even before I could reply, Mrs Surely stood up and dinged the bell behind her. This wasn't unusual. At our school the teachers sometimes made announcements at lunch like **"Football has been cancelled this afternoon because of the weather"** or **"Gemma Jamshed has been expelled for going behind the Big Hedge"**. Everyone went quiet.

Mrs Surely looked down at her notes.

"So..." she began. **"Today."** She shuffled her papers and cleared her throat. **"Today is World Book Day and−"**

She scratched her head with a finger. She gripped the

edge of the papers she was holding. She looked … well … a little confused.

All around the room, you could feel a tension taking hold. Mrs Surely was a confident, in-command sort of a teacher. Usually. She had an easy authority without needing to be horrible or angry. She was just someone who would say something and you would do it. It never really occurred to you not to listen to her, or not to obey her instructions. She was a good head teacher. She made you feel safe and in capable hands.

She never seemed nervous or hesitant or anxious, but suddenly she seemed to be all three of those things.

I leaned forward; the palms of my hands felt sweaty. I knew I was in danger – I was sure of it.

Mrs Surely lifted her right hand high into the air, fingers spread wide. She looked at it in bewilderment, as if she wasn't in charge of her own body. As if she was being manipulated by remote control.

Her thumb tucked on to her palm, then her little finger bent down.

"She's doing a countdown!" said Jezza quietly to himself.

Her ring finger folded down next, then her middle finger. Just one finger remained. It pointed upwards. Everyone in the dining hall held their breath. I felt light-headed but mesmerized. What was happening? What would happen when Mrs Surely got to zero?

She bent her last finger down, making a fist. She drew her arm in slightly, then straightened it again and silently punched the air.

I felt it before I heard it.

I've never been in an earthquake (luckily), but I bet it feels a little like what we experienced at that moment.

The entire building *quivered.* I can't think of a better word for it. It quivered. It buzzed. Like an electric toothbrush. Or like your cheeks when you hum at a certain pitch and your whole face vibrates and can sort of tickle if you do it right.

And we quivered too. The floor, the walls, my whole body trembled and shook. It was such a strong sensation I wondered if my teeth were going to be shaken right out of my head. My head shook so much my vision went blurry. To say it was a weird feeling hardly begins to do it justice.

And then the sound kicked in: a low, low tone. So low, so deep it took a while to pick it up. But as it rose in pitch I became aware of it and would have probably marvelled more at its awesome loudness and its powerful bass were it not for what all the teachers were doing.

Eyes closed, heads thrown back, the teachers rose slowly off their benches and into the air until

70

they were about a metre off the ground. All of them. Yes, up into the air and hovering there like it wasn't anything unusual, like it wasn't *against the laws of physics*, like gravity didn't exist. They hung in the air as if to say, *Everything you know about how the world works is wrong.* Mrs Surely, in front of them, fist still raised high in the air like some sort of salute, floated even higher than the others – her head thrown back as well, her eyes closed. It was as though they were in a trance.

The low throbbing noise grew louder. The room quivered more ferociously.

"**They're...**" began Leslie but had to stop.

"**They're...**" she tried again.

"**They're ... farting!**" I said, having the same realization at exactly the same time as Leslie.

Mrs Surely and all the teachers, about thirty of them, *were* farting. I was sure of it. But here's the strange thing... Let me rephrase that, because

everything happening was beyond strange...
Here's *another* incredibly strange thing – they
seemed to be farting *the same fart*.

It was as if they were all creating a single,
monstrous, giant, impossibly loud and impossibly
quivery fart. As if they were all contributing to it.
Or as if it was coming through them all at once.
As if they were being used to generate this thing,
this impossible, awesome, crazy thing that was

shaking this building and everyone in it.

I watched in horror as they hung in the air like birthday balloons: Miss Dollop, eyes closed, hands primly clasped in front of her, her floral skirt rippling in the … shall we say … *breeze*; Mr Ritter, a slight smile on his face; Mr Brown-Stain, his pinched face looking cross as usual.

And it just kept going – kept going for quite a long time but *thankfully* didn't seem to smell *at all*.

Slowly, the shock of what was happening began to fade slightly. I had, I realized, been standing there staring open-mouthed at the line of teachers hanging in mid-air. Now, for the first time, I looked around and could see that nearly every other pupil was doing the same.

And there in the corner were the two Ronnies I had seen earlier. At least I think they were – they could have been any two Ronnies… Anyway, two of the aliens stood holding an enormous version of the device I'd seen earlier and they were pointing it at the bottoms of the floating, farting teachers.

Jezza and Leslie were mesmerized by the sight – can you blame them? And Saskia… Saskia wasn't there. Saskia had vanished.

And so had Bonnie.

CHAPTER TEN

I ran down the corridor, not looking back, too scared, too hyped up. Without thinking, I ran straight back to our classroom and turned to see that Jezza and Leslie had followed and were right behind me.

We ran to our desks and sat down in our regular places. I don't know why we did that. I guess we were completely stressed out and not making clear and proper decisions. Or maybe we were hoping that if we pretended everything was normal, then it would *become* normal.

But all your teachers hovering off the ground, pumping out some kind of mega fart? Not normal. Not normal *at all*.

No one said anything for a bit, except Jezza, who kept shaking his head and saying, **"The noise. The noise of them all..."**

I was about to tell them about the sixty Ronnies and the ship when the door opened and Mr Brown-Stain walked in. Like I already told you at the very start, he behaved completely normally. After all that had happened that day, this seemed possibly the oddest thing yet.

He took off his jacket, kicked off his shoes, put on his tragic slippers, blew his nose, walked down the middle of the classroom, and between

Jezza's and Saskia's desks he fell forward on to his sizable nose with a *thunk*.

He lay there for what seemed like ages. Then the door opened and Miss Dollop came in and gasped. Mr Brown-Stain farted his ship's horn fart.

Immediately, a Ronnie came running in with one of their fart-sucking devices and pointed it at Mr Brown-Stain's bottom. Once the fart had finished, the Ronnie looked at Miss Dollop.

"**What?**" she said, alarmed.

"**Got something for me?**" asked Ronnie, not unpleasantly.

"I don't know what you mean," she protested.

"Better out than in," said Ronnie, giving her a knowing look.

"Don't," she squealed. "It's not lady-like."

"You will have to give in," Ronnie said. "I suggest sooner is better than later. This is the last. Then we have enough."

Miss Dollop, it was clear, was making an astonishing effort not to pass wind. She was clearly distressed at having publicly farted not once but twice already today, and she was doing heroic work now to stop her body doing what it was desperately trying to do.

Her face went red, then darker red, then purple. Her eyes watered, her hands shook, her face wobbled. But the little space pills that had been dropped into the teachers' food were clearly far too powerful to resist, and all at once *it happened.*

Boy, did it happen.

Forty seconds later, Ronnie pressed a few buttons on his machine and ran off.

"Come on!" I cried to Jezza and Leslie, giving chase, hoping and praying the others would follow.

CHAPTER ELEVEN

As we raced out of the classroom, the dining hall was emptying too. The sight of Ronnie belting across the playground with me in hot pursuit caused quite a commotion and I heard someone shouting my name. But this was not the time to stop for a chat.

Across the playground, behind the changing rooms, past the bins and over the football pitches, Ronnie raced to the hedge and I followed. Ronnie was quick, but he was also holding the device, which slowed him down. I was definitely gaining on him.

I could see he was thinking about going round the hedge, but with me so close he decided to go through it and he leapt at the bush to try and fly through in one mighty bound.

Which he did. He slipped right through the hedge, but the device didn't make it. He lost his grip on it as he disappeared into the greenery and the machine fell to the ground.

I picked it up, careful not to press any buttons or disturb it in any way, and as I began to squeeze through the hole Ronnie had made in the hedge, I heard it.

ChirrupChirrupChirrupChirrupChirrup
ChirrupChirrup Chirrup
Chirrup...

The sound of sixty

alarmed Ronnies excitedly chirruping.

And as I popped out of their side of the hedge, they stopped. Not gradually but suddenly. And there, in front of the spaceship, in a neat row, they stood: sixty Ronnies and Saskia Chintz.

"Saskia!" I exclaimed. "What are you doing?" I sounded like my mum when she catches me doing something I shouldn't be doing, like eating chocolate right before dinner, but I immediately realized that Saskia hadn't chosen to be here – she was being held against her will.

"We require the object you hold," said one of the Ronnies to me, pointing at the device. Was this their leader?

"I want my friend back," I replied. "Let's swap."

"Not possible," said the Ronnie. "We require her for our journey."

"Yes, but why?" said Saskia, as if she'd asked them this question several times and had not had a proper answer yet.

"For your talent," said Ronnie.

"Saskia?!" I said, shocked. "What talent?" Which came out all wrong and sounded like I thought she had no talents and couldn't believe she was worth kidnapping, but I didn't mean it like that. I just couldn't understand what talent she had that would be needed by a load of space Ronnies.

"Rude," said Saskia.

"Which specific talent?" I said, trying to back-pedal. "Which specific talent of her many, many talents?"

"Her ability to produce large-volume farts," said Ronnie.

"ALSO RUDE," said a very put-out-looking Saskia.

"Why do you need farts?" I asked. "Do you breathe them to stay alive?"

The Ronnies all looked offended.

"Of course not!" said the main Ronnie. "That is disgusting. We are not animals. The farts are fuel for our ship. We visited your planet and our research told us the Book World Day—"

"World Book Day."

"—yes – would be the best time to travel unnoticed. But your planet was further than we thought and Ronnie wanted to detour and stop on Saturn to view the rings –" he looked at another Ronnie who looked sheepish and blushed – "which we did not carry enough fuel to do. Your earth fartings are a perfect fuel for our ships, so we now have enough to get home if you give us the instrument you are holding.

Thanks you. Goodbye."

"Not unless you give me Saskia," I said, trying to sound like I had a confidence I didn't possess.

"No," said Ronnie. "She is a magnificent farter."

"STOP IT," said Saskia.

"She is back-up in case the fuel runs out," said Ronnie. "Please, the instrument."

"Listen," I said, trying to think quickly. "Listen. One of you was talking earlier about *The Wind in the Willows...*"

"Published in 1908," said all the Ronnies in unison.

"Yes," I said. "Published in 1908. It's a book about friends."

"A mole, a rat and a badger," they said, in unison once again.

"Yes and an annoying toad," I continued. "And they have good times and they have bad times, but even though they sometimes annoy each other and even though they fight and even though they bicker, ultimately they need each other and they look out for each other. Saskia is my friend, and even though she often annoys me and we often argue and myself and our classmates are well aware that she's a tremendous farter, I can't let anything bad happen to her because ... well ... because she's my friend."

The Ronnies stared at me and blinked. In unison.

"So I won't give you this instrument," I said, holding up the device, "unless you give me Saskia."

"Because of a talking rat and mole?"

"Kind of."

The sixty Ronnies went into a huddle. There was lots of chirruping, and after a while they formed a line again.

"We accept your deal," said Ronnie, "but I should warn you..."

He was interrupted by an avalanche of chirrups from the other Ronnies.

"**I think it's only fair to warn them!**" he exclaimed. They chirruped frantically back at him again.

"**OK,**" he conceded grumpily, "**I won't say anything. I suppose they'll discover it soon anyway.**"

What was he talking about?

He waved Saskia forward and I gave them the device. They loaded the teachers' farts into the spaceship, disappeared into a black tunnel and took off without another word or backward glance.

For a moment there was silence as Saskia and I watched their ship vanish into the clear blue sky without a sound and then a huge roar and cheer went up from the other side of the hedge. Saskia and I, confused, pushed through it to find the entire school gathered on the football pitch. They had been silently listening to everything that had gone on.

We didn't really know what to do. I didn't think I'd been all that much of a hero, and Saskia was a bit embarrassed that the whole school now knew she was capable of producing exceptionally large farts. That's not exactly the sort of thing you want to be known for, is it?

As the cheers subsided, we stood in stunned silence for a moment and I thought about Ronnie's comment: *I think it's only fair to warn them.* Warn us of what? Then in the distance the lesson bell sounded.

"**It's time for double maths,**" said Mr Brown-Stain. "**Off you go.**"

And I actually think he was serious.

THE END

Ready for more
out-of-this-world adventure?

THE FART THAT SAVED THE UNIVERSE

continues the story you've just read,
and is publishing on 8th May! Here's a
sneak peek...

CHAPTER ONE

You'd think, wouldn't you, that your friend would be pleased if you saved her from being abducted by aliens? You think she'd be pleased if you stopped her from being taken off into space never to be seen again?

Especially if the aliens only wanted your friend for her farting ability? Not because she was brainy or funny or amazing at music or a genius at art or anything. No! They wanted her because she had a "gift" for producing large amounts of gas from her bum. The aliens wanted her because, for them, farts are rocket fuel and they wanted her to power their spaceship back to their home planet.

But I stopped them. I saved my friend. I saved Saskia.

If someone had done that for me, how would I

have reacted?

Wow! Imagine!

I think I would have said thank you about four hundred and seventy million times. And then said it a few more times for good measure.

I think I'd have dedicated the rest of my life to repaying that person, knowing that THEY SAVED ME FROM BEING ABDUCTED BY ALIENS AND BEING TAKEN OFF INTO SPACE TO BE A HUMAN FART MACHINE AND THEY SAVED ME FROM NEVER BEING SEEN EVER AGAIN BY MY FRIENDS AND FAMILY.

So once the spacecraft had gone, once we'd watched it get smaller and smaller as it flew off into space and we saw it disappear into the pale blue sky that crazy day, once we'd all walked back in shocked silence to our classroom, once we'd sat down and looked around at each other in stunned amazement, Saskia turned to me and said,

"Why did you do that? Why didn't you let me

go with them? I'll never get the chance to fly in a spaceship ever again!"

What can you even say to that? I opened my mouth but nothing came out.

"I'll never get the chance to fly in a spaceship ever, ever again..." she repeated wistfully.

Turns out, though, she was wrong.

CHAPTER TWO

An emergency assembly was called. I would have just sent us all home for a week's holiday to get over the whole thing, but teachers love assemblies. I reckon they call them as often as they can get away with.

Think about it: when teachers are sitting in assemblies they can just sit there. They don't have to teach anything, they don't have to set tests, they don't have to mark homework.

"Maybe they'll send us home with instructions just to lounge about relaxing and eating sweets until we feel more normal?" I whispered to Jezza Tuesday, more in hope than expectation. When had a head teacher ever given any of the children in their school that kind of order in the whole history of schools? Probably never. But then when had a spaceship ever landed behind a big hedge near the football pitch at a school before? Also probably never.

It was odd watching the teachers troop into the main hall because the last time we'd seen them together they'd been hovering off the ground in a line, farting violently. It's not easy to forget an image like that and from the faces of the other pupils around me it was clear that no one had. There was an uncomfortable atmosphere in the room as if no one knew how to react to what had happened. It had been so weird. I kept a close eye on Miss Dollop, the art teacher. She'd been one of the most productive farters, which was as shocking as it had been surprising. She certainly looked embarrassed now and kept her eyes firmly fixed on the ground.

"Doubt it," whispered Jezza back glumly.

"They'll probably want us to catch up on the lessons we missed."

Mrs Surely, the head teacher, stood up and everyone fell silent.

"It's been an eventful day," she began. "An unusual day. Not the sort of day we had any plans for. We imagine what to do if a fire breaks out or if the heating breaks down or if lots of teachers suddenly fall ill, but we never imagined a day when an alien spacecraft would land and aliens would secretly slip space beans into our food and then harvest our ... collect our..." She trailed off. She didn't want to use the word "farts" and everyone in the room knew it.

She tried again.

"**They made us...**" But she couldn't do it so she moved on. "**And it is thanks to the bravery and clever thinking of some of you that a major crisis was averted.**"

Everyone turned to look at me and I actually blushed. Like properly went red in the face and felt suddenly hot. I didn't know what I was supposed to do. Get up and punch the air? Bow? Salute? In the end I just grinned and then frowned and felt hot and red and uncomfortable.

"**So we are going to end school a little early,**" continued Mrs Surely. "**We'll call your parents and caregivers and I suggest you all go home and relax and maybe even treat yourselves to a packet of sweets or a bar of chocolate. I know I will be. We'll see you all in the morning.**"

I was gobsmacked. She had actually suggested we go home, do nothing and eat sweets! What an incredible day! I felt like asking her to put it in writing so I could show my mum because I wasn't sure she'd believe me.

Saskia, Jezza and our other friend Leslie Grunt-Licker and I were the last to leave the main hall. It was hard to stand up. All that adrenaline, all the excitement of the day seemed suddenly to crash in on us and we just sat there as everyone got up and left.

We were in a kind of daze.

"Come on," said Jezza after a while. **"Those sweets won't eat themselves."**

We ambled silently out of the room, across the entrance lobby and through the double glass doors that opened out towards the school playground. A little kid, dressed in an anorak with the hood up came charging through, in such a rush that he smacked into me, almost knocking me over.

"Watch it!" I blurted out.

"I am sorry for the collision!" he called and

rushed off.

All four of us froze to the spot. All four of us recognized that voice. All four of us instantly knew who was hidden under that anorak.

"Ronnie!" I gasped.

"Yes!" breathed Saskia.

"Definitely!" said Leslie.

"Or Bonnie!" said Jezza, a little annoyingly.

Either way, one alien was still here! Why? How? Had they been left behind?

One thing was certain – all four of us made exactly the same split decision at exactly the same moment and, without saying a word, we turned and rushed after the little figure as it flung open the doors into the main hall.

We burst into the big empty room, but Ronnie (or Bonnie) was nowhere to be seen. Where could they have gone?

I was about to suggest we spread out and search

when up they popped from behind the upright piano by the wall and headed sharply for the exit.

"Wait!" shouted Saskia. "Please wait!"

The alien stopped and turned to face us.

"Good day! Good afternoon! Good evening! Nice weather we are having for the time of year!" It bowed and turned to leave again.

"Please stop!" called Saskia, the desperation clear in her voice. We all ran towards Ronnie/Bonnie. "What are you doing here?"

The alien stopped again. I noticed it was holding a piece of clothing.

"It's OK," I said, seeing that the little thing was clearly quite anxious.

"I forgot my jumper," said the creature, blinking nervously. "It was a present for my birthday and my mum would kill me if I went home without it. She knitted it for me. It doesn't really fit properly but I can't tell her that as she'll get too upset."

"So you turned the spaceship around and came back?!" said Saskia incredulously.

"Yes," said the alien. "Everyone was very annoyed at me for that but at least I remembered just after we'd left and not when we got all the way back home."

"The spaceship is here again?!" said Saskia. "In the same place?"

Ronnie/Bonnie nodded and Saskia, without saying another word, turned and ran as fast as she could out of the main hall.

I looked to Leslie and Jezza and knew they were thinking the same thing I was: Saskia was going to try to get on board that spaceship. She was obsessed. She had to be stopped.

"Come on," I said to Ronnie/Bonnie. "We'll help you get back to your spaceship."

CHAPTER THREE

Luckily the playground was almost empty. If you tell children to leave school and go home to eat sweets then they will do just that and they will do it as quickly as humanly possible.

We surrounded the little alien, who had his hood pulled low over his face, and jogged down to the football pitch.

"I should be at home eating chocolate by now," grumbled Jezza. "If Saskia's daft enough to get on that ship and fly off with these weird creatures, no offence, Ronnie, then that's her lookout."

"We can't let her!" I protested. "She hasn't thought it through. They're not going to drop her back home when she's had enough. If she gets on that ship she'll never come back again. Ever!"

"And who know what other problems she'll have?" said Leslie. "She might catch a freaky space disease.

Or get space sickness. Or alien fever. Or some sort of Ronnie rash. We don't know where these aliens have been!"

Leslie was always imagining that she was going to catch some disease or other and took great pains to stay clean. She only ever used the school loos if she was absolutely desperate, she always wiped down her chair in a classroom with an antiseptic wipe before sitting down (**"Someone else's bum has been on that!"**) and if she heard that anyone in any class in the whole school had a cold or the flu or a stomach bug then she'd go immediately to the school nurse because she would be convinced that she had it too.

She once overheard Gary Niblet in the class above us say that his dog had fleas and she rushed to the school nurse because she said she felt itchy all over and reckoned she must have fleas too.

Nearly every morning she'd come to school and tell us that she'd probably caught some condition or other: measles, mumps, leprosy, gout – you name it, she's been convinced at some point that she's had it.

Across the football pitch we ran, scrambled through the hedge and there it was: Ronnie's ship. As big as three double-decker buses and so black it was hard to look at. Light seemed to disappear into it and not come out again. No windows that I could see, no doors, no sign of Saskia.

"Saskia!" I shouted.

"Please do not be shouting!" implored Ronnie/ Bonnie. "I am already in trouble with everyone for making them come back. I must go."

"Is Saskia on your ship?" I asked quickly. Ronnie/Bonnie's eyes narrowed, he placed a hand to his forehead, then looked up and pointed. A square section of the huge black side of the ship, high up on the right-hand side, switched from solid to see-through and there was Saskia, surrounded by a group of aliens, talking and waving her arms around. What was she doing!?

"**Goodbye, thank you, goodbye,**" said Ronnie/ Bonnie as he scuttled towards the middle of the ship.

"**We have to stop Saskia,**" I blurted to Jezza and Leslie.

"**How?**" said Jezza.

"**We have to get her off the ship. Come on!**" I ran to follow Ronnie/Bonnie, who was now nearly at the ship.

"**I'm not going near that!**" shrieked Leslie. "**Can you even imagine how dirty it is?**"

"Then don't," I said, "but Saskia is my friend and I'm not going to let her make the biggest mistake of her life and fly off with a load of aliens just because she wants to see what space is like. I'm going after her!" I turned, put my head down and charged forward towards the little doorway that Ronnie/Bonnie was slipping through. If I didn't get to it in time there was every chance that the door would close, the spaceship would fire up its engines and take off away into space with Saskia on board.

I was screaming; Leslie was screaming; Jezza was screaming. With Ronnie/Bonnie now inside the ship, the door started to close. With a last mighty effort, I lunged for the entrance to block the door and prevent it from shutting, but in that moment I was stronger than I realized and I yanked Leslie and Jezza and myself right through the narrow doorway where we collapsed on to the floor in a heap. The door slammed shut behind us, the spaceship fired up its engines, and before I could speak or think or react or do anything, it lifted off the ground and faster than a speeding bullet shot up towards the dark inky blackness of space.

WHAT'S IT LIKE WORKING TOGETHER AS BROTHER AND SISTER?

ANITA: It's lovely! I spend a lot of time rolling on the floor laughing at Stephen's hilarious words.

STEPHEN: Fun! Anita's drawings really make me laugh.

WHAT WAS THEIR MOST ANNOYING HABIT GROWING UP?

STEPHEN: She really wasn't that annoying, but if we were in the car in the countryside and there were any "countryside" smells she'd completely freak out!

ANITA: On long car journeys Stephen would place his finger on my shoulder for AGES just to annoy me!

TELL US A SURPRISE ABOUT YOUR NEXT BOOK.

ANITA: If I told you, it wouldn't be a surprise!

STEPHEN: It's got a waiter who is a huge moustache with a tiny creature attached to the top of it.

WHO'S YOUR FAVOURITE CHARACTER IN THE BOOK?

STEPHEN: Mr Wojciechowski is my favourite character (even though he's quite grumpy) because he knows all the best books. He just needs to use a different shampoo.

ANITA: I like all the Ronnies – oh oops, that's more than one...

WHAT WOULD YOU DO IF YOU BLASTED OFF INTO SPACE AND COULD VISIT ANY PLANET?

ANITA: I would like to go on a universe tour of all of them, with time sped up so that we could go to all of them and get home in time for dinner.

STEPHEN: Have a look on Space Trip Advisor for the most highly recommended ones and go there.

WHY SHOULD YOU READ *THE FART THAT SAVED THE UNIVERSE*?

STEPHEN: So that you know what to do if you ever need to fart to save the universe.

ANITA: Because you NEED to find out what happens! AND it's a great story and very, very funny.

STEPHEN MANGAN is a bestselling author, script-writer and actor across TV, radio, film and theatre. He is well-known for acclaimed comedy, drama and presenting series like *Portrait Artist of the Year* and *The Fortune Hotel*. Stephen regularly appears on stage and has played *Ebeneezer Scrooge* in *A Christmas Carol*. Stephen also voiced the title role in *Postman Pat: The Movie*. He has been a judge for the Costa Book of the Year prize and the Laugh Out Loud Book Awards (the Lollies). His first book was *Escape the Rooms*, illustrated by Anita Mangan.

ANITA MANGAN is a celebrated graphic designer and illustrator. She has designed or illustrated over 90 books including two of her own: *Bingo, An Illustrated Guide to Bingo Lingo* and *The Chinese Zodiac, A Seriously Silly Guide*. She was a judge for the Lollies Awards in 2023 and has appeared on *Celebrity Portrait Artist of the Year* and *Celebrity Gogglebox*. She can mostly be found in her studio at the bottom of the garden surrounded by thousands of tiny colourful objects and with her dog, Dusty, under her desk.

DON'T MISS...

HAPPY WORLD BOOK DAY

Choosing to read in your free time can help make you:

Feel happier

Better at reading

More successful

Whether it's **comics**, **audiobooks**, **recipe books** or **non-fiction** you can visit your school, local library or nearest bookshop for your next read.

Keep the reading fun going by **swapping** this book, **talking** about it, or **reading it again!**

Discover more at worldbookday.com

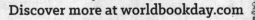

READ YOUR WAY

Celebrate World Book Day by reading what YOU want in YOUR free time.

World Book Day® is a charity sponsored by National Book Tokens.